The Two Tims

To best friends everywhere
D. E.

For my brother and best mate, Pete
G. A.

Text copyright © 2016 by David Elliott
Illustrations copyright © 2016 by Gabriel Alborozo

First edition 2016

Library of Congress Catalog Card Number 2015934468
ISBN 978-0-7636-7264-5

16 17 18 19 20 21 CCP 10 9 8 7 6 5 4 3 2 1

Printed in Shenzhen, Guangdong, China

This book was typeset in Anke Sans.
The illustrations were done in pen and ink and colored digitally.

Candlewick Press
99 Dover Street
Somerville, Massachusetts 02144

visit us at www.candlewick.com

The Two Tims

illustrated by

David Elliott   Gabriel Alborozo

CANDLEWICK PRESS

Look, everybody! It's Tim!

Hi, Tim!

Hey! This is Tim, too!

What's up, Tim?

Two Tims.

Best friends.

Wherever Tim goes, there goes Tim.

Whatever Tim does, Tim does it, too.

Two Tims. Best friends.
Forever.

Until Tom comes along.

Tom likes to play knights.
So does Tim.

Tim doesn't.
Tim thinks knights are boring!

Tom likes to crazy-dance. Tim does, too.

Not Tim.

And Tom likes to swim.

Tim doesn't know how.
Neither does Tim.

And he does.

Two Tims and a Tom.

Best friends.

Forever.